Parmesan Pizza Murder

Papa Pacelli's Pizzeria Series

Book Sixteen

By

Patti Benning

Author's Note: On the next page, you'll find out how to access all of my books easily, as well as locate books by best-selling author, Summer Prescott. I'd love to hear your thoughts on my books, the storylines, and anything else that you'd like to comment on – reader feedback is very important to me. Please see the following page for my publisher's contact information. If you'd like to be on her list of "folks to contact" with updates, release and sales notifications, etc...just shoot her an email and let her know. Thanks for reading!

Also...

...if you're looking for more great reads, from me and Summer, check out the Summer Prescott Publishing Book Catalog:

http://summerprescottbooks.com/book-catalog/ for some truly delicious stories.

Contact Info for Summer Prescott Publishing:

Twitter: @summerprescott1

Blog and Book Catalog: http://summerprescottbooks.com

Email: summer.prescott.cozies@gmail.com

And…look up The Summer Prescott Fan Page and Summer Prescott Publishing Page on Facebook – let's be friends!

To sign up for our fun and exciting newsletter, which will give you opportunities to win prizes and swag, enter contests, and be the first to know about New Releases, click here:

https://forms.aweber.com/form/02/1682036602.htm

Acknowledgement

Many thanks to Michelle Mabry who suggested the delicious cauliflower crust pizza. It's one of the best alternatives to a normal pizza crust that I've ever had. I recommend it to anyone who's looking to enjoy a pizza without all of the carbs. Who would have thought that eating pizza could be so healthy?

TABLE OF CONTENTS

PARMESAN PIZZA
MURDER

Papa Pacelli's Pizzeria Series Book Sixteen

CHAPTER ONE

"This should be the last bag," Eleanora Pacelli said. "It took a while, but it needed to be done."

Jacob, one of the two employees that had been at Papa Pacelli's longer than she had, opened the large black garbage bag while Ellie swept the last few leaves into a pile. The parking lot and sidewalk behind the pizzeria looked much better now, though she knew it would only be a matter of time before more leaves fell and cluttered the area they had just cleaned.

"Just in time, there's Sabrina," Jacob said. Ellie straightened up and waved to her newest employee, the pretty young woman whom she had hired shortly after one of her other employees had left to work for someone else in town. Sabrina had proven herself to be a quick learner and a reliable worker, and Ellie hoped that she would work at the pizzeria for a long time to come. Employees could make or break a restaurant, and good ones could be hard to come by.

Sabrina pulled her car into one of the employee parking spots and got out. "Do the two of you need help?" she asked.

"No, we're just about done," Ellie said. "You can take a short break until the next delivery order is ready, if you'd like."

"Thanks, Ms. P.," Sabrina said. "It will be nice to be out of the car for a bit."

Ellie helped Jacob finish up the leaves, sweeping the last of them into the bag. As she was tying the top of the full bag shut, she saw another familiar vehicle pull into the pizzeria's parking lot.

The sheriff parked his truck under the sparse shade of a tree that had already begun to lose its leaves. Ellie headed towards him, making a quick detour to drop the garbage bag in the dumpster. She grinned when she saw her fiancé, Russell Ward, get out of the vehicle.

"I just thought I'd stop by and say hi," he said. "I'm on my way back to the sheriff's department now, then I'll be free for the night. Liam's going to be working evenings for a while, which will be a nice change."

"Too bad the pizzeria doesn't close until late," she said. "Otherwise we might actually have been able to start eating dinner together on a regular basis."

12

"At least now I'll be able to stop in and bring you a coffee," he said. "You've done the same for me enough times."

"That would be very much appreciated," Ellie said. "Even if you don't bring coffee, feel free to stop in anytime you want. It's always nice to see you."

He smiled. "While I've got you here, what would you say about going to dinner –"

The pizzeria owner held up her hand, grimacing apologetically. Her phone had just started ringing, and she was waiting for a call from the woman running the second pizzeria down in Florida. They were only weeks away from their grand opening, and she had to take it.

"Hi, Linda," she said, pressing the phone to her ear. "How did the interview go?"

"I really liked her," the other woman said. "I wanted to talk to Sandra about it first, but I think I'll be calling her back tomorrow to tell her she's hired."

"Wonderful," Ellie said. "Her resume looked promising. Hiring another employee was the last major thing on the list, which means that we're just about ready to open. Have you set aside time to train everyone? I know Sandra's been a great help, but she still needs to learn her way around a restaurant."

"Yes. Once we hire the new girl, I'll set up a schedule for training. I've already set aside the weekend before the grand opening to do a final run-through and make sure things are running smoothly."

"Good. How has advertising been going?"

"We've had some interest; mainly from my previous customers, who are excited that the restaurant is going to be reopening even if it's under another name."

"That's good, but we really need more people to be interested. I'll email –"

Russell tapped on the shoulder, interrupting her. "I'm going to head to the sheriff's department and check in with Liam so I can head home," he said quietly. "I'll call you later."

She smiled and gave him a quick kiss before turning her attention back to Linda. "Sorry about that. I'll email some of the local papers down there and see if they can run ads for us over the next few weeks. You can print out more flyers and ask if you can hang them up in some of the other small businesses around town. Feel free to give the people working there a couple of coupons for discounted pizzas. It will help get the word out, which is the most important thing right now."

"Okay. I can't believe it's almost time to open it. Six months ago, I thought I was going to have to shut down the restaurant for good. I know I've said it before, but thank you, Ellie. This really means a lot to me. I'll do my best, I promise."

Ellie said her goodbyes and hung up. Arranging things for the second pizzeria had been her number one priority recently. Linda was a good cook, but wasn't experienced in running a business. The little pizzeria that she had been struggling to keep open a few months ago had been her husband's, who had passed away a couple of years beforehand. The food itself was good, but her business model had not been, and she had been only a few short weeks away from being forced to permanently close the doors.

After meeting the woman during her trip to Florida, Ellie had decided to extend her an offer to buy the building and help her reopen it under Papa Pacelli's name. The interior of the building had been completely redesigned to match the decor and old timey pizzeria feel of the original Papa Pacelli's in Kittiport, and they would be using Arthur Pacelli's secret crust recipe, but other than that, she was giving the other woman a lot of freedom to do what she wanted with the restaurant. She just hoped that Linda would be

able to keep up with it and wouldn't make any major errors that
would cost the business money.

Trying to put the other pizzeria out of her mind temporarily, Ellie
looked around and realized that Russell was gone. She remembered
hearing him say that he was leaving, but somehow it hadn't quite
registered in her brain. She felt a stab of guilt. She hadn't been
giving him the attention that he deserved. Russell had come through
for her so many times, and here she was ignoring him while she
fielded a call from Linda. Linda could have waited the few minutes
it would have taken to say a proper goodbye to her fiancé.

I'll make it up to him later, she promised herself. *I'll set aside time
for a nice dinner together, and I'll remind him that all of this
busyness is only temporary.*

Resolving to do a better job of not letting her loved ones come in
second place to work, Ellie tucked her cell phone back in her pocket
and went inside. Even though it had been stressful rushing to get
everything set up on time, she shared Linda's excitement for the
opening of the second pizzeria. If Papa Pacelli's did as well down
in Florida as it was doing in Maine, then the pizzeria would truly be
on its way to fame.

She went back inside, finding Sabrina up front, chatting with one of
her friends. She had seen the young woman a couple of times before;

16

all of her employees had friends that came in a couple of times a week. Ellie didn't mind. They almost always bought something, and as long as her employees didn't neglect their work, it didn't bother her if they took a few minutes every now and then to talk to someone they knew.

"Hi, Sadie," she said, giving the young woman a smile so she would know she was welcome. "It's good to see you again."

"You too, Ms. Pacelli."

Ellie settled down behind the register, already thinking about new ways they could advertise the second pizzeria. They were in the home run; in just a few weeks, all of her hard work would pay off and life would be back to normal.

PATTI BENNING

CHAPTER TWO

Keeping true to her promise, Ellie scheduled herself for a couple of hours off that Thursday so she could spend the evening with Russell. She brought a pizza and a two liter of soda over to his house, along with a couple of movies that they had both been wanting to watch. He let her into the house and greeted her with a hug. She put the food on the table before bending down to pet his cat, Sookie. The little tabby began to purr and arched her back, happy as could be with the attention. Ellie smiled. The cat had been the one to adopt Russell, instead of the other way around. One day, Sookie had simply appeared on his doorstep and had refused to leave ever since. It was good for Russell to have another living being in his house, even it was a six-pound ball of fluff.

Russell's house was one of the smaller, older ones in a sparsely populated neighborhood on the outskirts of town. He had been renting it for the past few years, ever since he had sold the house he had shared with his deceased wife. Ellie had always liked going over there, and always felt at home the second she stepped through the door.

"So, how is everything going with the restaurant in Florida?" he asked as they sat down for their meal.

"It's... going," Ellie said. "Between Linda, Sandra, and the girl we just hired, we've got all the employees we'll need for the first few months, unless it's even busier than we expect it to be. All of the appliances are installed, and we've got our deliveries from our suppliers set up. She needs to advertise more, which I'm going to be helping her with this weekend. We need people to be excited about this pizzeria. It's not like Kittiport, where we're the only pizza place in town. In Miami, there are hundreds of other pizzerias to choose from. We need to give people a reason to choose Papa Pacelli's in particular."

"It's a big jump for you," he said. "Going from running such a comfortable small-town eatery to something in a major city across the country."

"The goal is for Linda to manage almost everything on her own eventually," Ellie said. "I wasn't planning on making such a big leap, but then I met her. She needed the help, and she already has some experience with the business. It just seemed to fit."

PARMESAN PIZZA MURDER: PAPA PACELLI'S PIZZERIA SERIES BOOK SIXTEEN

"Well, if anyone to make it work, you can."

"Thanks," she said, giving him a smile. "How are things going for you? I feel like we're always talking about my work, but we never really discuss yours."

"Well, nothing much changes for me," he said. "I like it that way. It's always a good thing when the town is quiet. I like not having to do more than hand out the occasional speeding ticket."

"Kittiport is a good town," Ellie said. "And the people are lucky to have you as their sheriff. I think you're almost as well-known as the mayor is."

He chuckled. "Well, I don't do it for the publicity. I just like helping people, and have lived in this town for my whole life. For as long as I'm able to take care of it, I want to."

"It must be wonderful to have a place where you feel so deeply at home," she said with a sigh. "Between moving away from here and bouncing around Chicago for most of my life, sometimes it feels like I don't really have a place like that."

"Kittiport will be that place for you," he said. "You already have roots here, even if you haven't been here your entire life. Home doesn't have to be where you have spent most of your time. It's where your loved ones are, and where your heart is."

After dinner, Russell locked up his house and the two of them set off together to walk along the quiet streets. It was evening, mostly dark already, and the street lights were on, the orange glow illuminating the sidewalk. They walked hand-in-hand, and Ellie felt happy and at peace in a way that she didn't remember feeling very often before.

"It's a beautiful night," she said.

"Beautiful, but chilly," Russell replied. "Winter is on its way."

Winter, Ellie thought. For her, winter and the holiday season were only vague ideas. She was completely focused on the upcoming grand opening and her trip to Florida in just a couple of weeks. She, Russell, her grandmother, and the entire team of employees at the pizzeria were going down there for the weekend. It would be a grand opening in the truest sense, and would hopefully help to bind the two restaurants together. Even though they were separated by distance, she wanted both teams to feel like family.

"You okay?"

"Yes," she said. "Just thinking about the pizzeria again."

"I'm sure you'll be happier once it's open and doing well," he said. "Let's cross here."

They turned to cross the road, but had to pause to let a car go by. Ellie did a double take when she saw the lighted sign on top that read *Pizza*. She frowned, her gaze following the car as it made its way down the block and pulled into someone's driveway. She saw a person get out of the vehicle carrying a pizza box, knock on the door, and trade the box for money before getting back into the vehicle. The car headed away from them in the opposite direction.

Russell, who had been watching the vehicle's progress with her, squeezed her hand. "Is everything all right?"

"I just didn't think anyone else delivered all the way out here," she said. "The closest pizza place I know of, other than Papa Pacelli's, is in Benton Harbor. Why would they deliver to Kittiport at almost ten-thirty on a Thursday night?"

"Maybe they changed their schedule to be open later than Papa Pacelli's," he suggested. "It might be worth it for them to deliver a little bit further out, if they're the only place around here that's open this late."

"I suppose," she said with a frown. It wasn't that she minded the competition. It was just that she had enough on her plate without having to think about what it would mean if she had to extend her business hours even more just to keep the pizzeria in Benton Harbor from gaining a foothold here in Kittiport. Whatever they were doing, it could wait until after the second pizzeria's opening. Surely a couple of weeks couldn't make that much difference.

CHAPTER THREE

Friday evenings were always one of the busiest times at Papa Pacelli's, even more so now that the local schools had started back up and there were football games many of the Friday evenings. That particular evening, they were working on a bulk order for the local high school football teams. Ten pizzas, two of which had to be vegetarian, along with a few orders of breadsticks, and a hefty amount of two-liter sodas. This was on top of all of the normal orders, which meant that the kitchen was being pushed to its limit. Unlike some of the larger chains, each and every pizza at Papa Pacelli's was made from scratch. With only two ovens, each of which could fit two pizzas at a time, it took quite a while to get an order that big out and ready for delivery.

"Are you sure you don't want me to send someone else along to help?" Ellie asked as she watched Sabrina load up her car.

"I think I'll be able to manage, Ms. P.," the woman said.

"Okay, just take your time. I told them it would be a while, so you don't have to rush to get there.

Sabrina drove away, the cargo of pizzas and drinks secure in the back of her car. Ellie watched her go, then hurried back inside. None of them would be getting much of a break that evening, though she was hoping to be able to grab a few minutes to eat some dinner of her own. Having a growling stomach took some of the enjoyment out of making food for others, and she hadn't eaten since brunch earlier in the day.

She got her chance when Shannon and James Ward – Russell's brother and sister-in-law — stopped in an hour later for dinner. Ellie was thrilled to see them. She hadn't been able to spend as much time with her friend recently as she would've liked, and knew that Shannon probably had a lot to tell her. Her friend had recently found out that she was pregnant, and was both terrified and thrilled at the thought of having a child later in life. Ellie knew that it wasn't that uncommon for older woman to have a child these days, but she was worried for her friend, not only because of all of the possible health issues that could arise, but because the other woman's life was going to change, and drastically, for the next eighteen years, and she didn't know if Shannon was completely prepared for it.

"What can I get the two of you tonight?" she asked, stopping by the table with a pen and a pad of paper. Usually, she memorized the orders, but that evening was chaotic enough that she was worried about forgetting something important.

"Ellie!" Shannon said, looking thrilled to see her. "We were wondering if you'd be able to come out of the kitchen and see us yourself. It's busy in here tonight."

"Yeah, a lot of people stopped by after the game," Ellie said.

"That's actually where we're coming from," Shannon said. "I've got to write an article about it for tomorrow's paper. We won, as you've probably heard about a hundred times by now."

"Yes, people have been talking about it all evening," Ellie said. Another small group of people came in. Shannon saw her glance over at them.

"Sorry, we shouldn't be keeping you," her friend said. "I'll have a personal size spinach and artichoke pizza with white sauce and extra cheese."

"I'd just like a pepperoni pizza, also personal sized," James said.

"You got it," Ellie said. "Anything to drink?"

"Just water," Shannon said. "I'm trying to be healthier; I don't want to my little one addicted to sugar and caffeine before he's even born."

"He'll have plenty of time for that when he's older," she replied, grinning. "Do you know the gender yet?"

"Not yet. It will be another couple of weeks until the doctor will be able to tell. I just don't feel right calling him 'it' until then, and I have a lot of the same early pregnancy symptoms that James's mom did both times she had the boys. We'll be happy either way."

"Of course," Ellie said. "I can't wait to hear the news when you find out."

"Aunt Ellie will be the first to know," Shannon said, grinning.

"Your kid will have free pizzas for life," she promised. "I'd better get back to the kitchen, but if you don't mind, I'll come back when your pizzas are done and join you for a few minutes. I haven't gotten a chance to eat yet this evening, and a quick dinner with the two of you beats standing over the sink in the kitchen with a slice of pizza."

"Perfect," Shannon said. "When you come back, maybe we can talk about my baby shower. I want to start planning it, but I need to make sure you'll be able to come."

"As long as it's after the trip to Florida, any time is good for me."

She returned to the kitchen and began working on her soon-to-be in-laws' orders. As she was putting the two personal pizzas in the oven, Sabrina returned to pick up the next couple delivery orders.

"Only an hour left before we close," she said, trying to encourage her tired employee. "You've been great tonight."

"Thanks, Ms. P., it's been a busy evening. It will be nice to sleep in tomorrow."

"Definitely," agreed Ellie, who was very much not a morning person. "Drive safely. We'll stop taking delivery orders pretty soon, so you should only need to make one more trip after this."

On her way back to the kitchen, she was waylaid by someone else. It was a young man who she knew she had seen around before, but didn't know him well enough to put a name to his face.

"Excuse me, Ms. Pacelli?"

"Yes?"

"My name's Kyle Hart. I was wondering if I could get an application."

"Sorry," she said. "We aren't hiring right now." Someone jostled her as they pushed past. "And it's a really busy night. Come back some other time and we can talk about it. We may need someone for the holidays."

"I will. Sorry to bother you. Thanks."

She gave him a strained smile and then pushed her way through the line to the door behind the register. Being busy was a good thing, but sometimes it had its downfalls.

While Shannon and James' pizzas cooked, she pulled the large everything pizza that her employees had been snacking on all evening out of the fridge. There were four pieces left, and she put two on a small pan and stuck it in the oven underneath the two small pizzas to reheat it. Her stomach rumbled. Food, at last, and only an hour left of work — not counting the cleaning that would have to be done before closing, but she didn't mind that. She was exhausted, but she felt satisfied knowing that their hard work had resulted in a lot of happy customers. The pizzeria was more popular than ever, and her employees worked together with the ease of a well-oiled machine. What more could she ask for?

As if her thoughts had jinxed things, Rose came into the kitchen with the pizzeria's phone in her hand. "Someone's calling to change an order that I don't have any record of them placing in the first place," her employee said. "What should I do?"

"I'll take it," Ellie said with a sigh. "You handle things in here for a second, okay?" It was a busy evening indeed, and football season had just started. Maybe she should have given Kyle that application. If tonight was any indication, they might be able to use the extra help.

Twenty minutes later, just as she was picking up her plate and preparing to leave the table where she had eaten with Shannon and James, Rose, who was working the register, called her over.

"Ms. P., someone's on hold. They said they wanted to speak with you, specifically," she said.

"All right," the pizzeria owner said. "I'll be right there."

"It sounded important," her employee said.

With a sigh, Ellie set her plate back down and headed over to the counter. "Hello?" she asked, taking the phone from Rose.

"Ellie?" It was a man's voice, but she couldn't place it.

"Yes? Who is this?"

"Ellie, this is Liam," he said. "I hate making this call, but I knew you would want to hear it here before you hear it from someone else."

"What happened?" she asked, feeling her stomach lurch. Had something happened to Russell?

"I'm still at the scene of the accident," he said. She felt her lungs stop working when she heard that word. Accident. "I'm so sorry, Ellie, but your employee — a Ms. Sabrina Williams — is dead."

CHAPTER FOUR

The first thing that she felt was relief, and she didn't know if she would ever be able to forgive herself for that. *It's not Russell.* Then she felt the horror, rising anew within her. Sabrina was dead. How was that possible? She had seen the young woman not even half an hour ago. She had seen her, looking tired, walking out the door to drive through town at night... "Oh my goodness," she breathed, leaning heavily against the counter.

Rose shot her a concerned look, her mouth opening as if to ask what was going on, then shutting again, evidently deciding that it wasn't her place to pry. Ellie blinked, realizing that Liam was still talking, but she hadn't heard his last few sentences.

"Where is she?" she asked.

"A house on Green Street," he said. "The homeowner confirmed that she was there to deliver a pizza. We aren't sure what happened, yet. It looks like it could have been a hit and run. She was found in the road —"

"She wasn't in her car?"

"No."

She didn't crash, Ellie thought. *Someone did this to her.*

"Did you call Russell?"

"I left him a message. It's his night off. He probably isn't —"

She cut him off again. "I'm coming there. I want to see... I don't know what I'm expecting to see, but I want to be there. She wouldn't have been out there if it wasn't for me."

"No, Ellie —"

Ellie let her arm holding the phone fall to her side, pressing the red button to end the call as she did so. She looked at Rose, who was frowning at her with real concern now. What did her face look like? She couldn't feel her muscles; couldn't tell what sort of expression she was making.

"Rose, start closing down the pizzeria. Sabrina's been in an accident. I'll call you as soon as I know more. I have to go now."

She hurried through the kitchen, grabbing her purse and pulling her keys out as she left through the pizzeria's back door, ignoring her employee's concerned shouts after her. She had forgotten Shannon and James, who were still sitting at the table in the dining area. She could hardly believe this was real. She hadn't known Sabrina well, but she had liked her, and more importantly, she had been responsible for her. How could this have happened?

She felt a sudden burning anger directed at whoever had hit the young woman with their car. If the person had stayed to help or had made a call to 911 after the accident, she was sure Liam would have mentioned it. The way he had said it, it sounded like someone had simply found her in the road after the accident occurred. That meant that someone had hit a young, twenty-year-old girl with their vehicle, and had driven away without doing anything to help her afterward.

She hadn't been in Kittiport long enough to have all of the roads memorized, but she knew where Green Street was. It was one of the nicer residential streets in town, and she often drove down it when she was visiting Shannon.

It was easy to find the location of the accident. The sight of the ambulance sitting in the street with its lights flashing made her stomach drop. She knew that if Sabrina had been alive when it got there, it would have taken off to the nearest hospital as soon as the paramedics had loaded her onto the stretcher. Now, with her declared dead, there was no rush, and the paramedics were talking to the police.

She recognized Liam's cruiser. The second one likely belonged to the other deputy, Bethany. She looked for Russell's truck, but didn't see it. He wasn't there yet. There was a small group of people standing on the sidewalk, staring at the scene and talking quietly among themselves. Sabrina's car, with the pizza delivery sign on top, was still parked along the curb.

Ellie pulled to a stop a couple of yards away from the police and got out of her car. Liam looked up, and she could tell that he recognized her even from that distance. He said something, and Bethany turned and hurried towards her.

"Ellie, Liam didn't mean for you to drive out here," she said. "Since you're here, you should sit down. Would you mind waiting in your car? He's trying to gather information from everyone who might have seen something. We're still not sure what happened."

"I thought it was an accident?" Ellie said.

"No, it wasn't," Bethany said. "Liam said he thought so at first, but the paramedics determined that her injuries weren't consistent with a car accident. A fatal head injury was the cause of death, but we're not sure from what."

"So, this wasn't an accident?" the pizzeria owner said. "Someone did this to her on purpose?" She realized that her hands were shaking. All of this was too much to take in. How could any of this have happened?

"Like I said, we aren't sure what happened yet," the younger woman said. She placed her hand on Ellie's shoulder. "Russell will be here soon. Since it's an active crime scene, I'd appreciate it if you waited back here. You don't have to stay in your car, but I'm sure it would be more comfortable."

"Of course," she replied. "I'm sorry. Maybe I shouldn't have come, but I just had to see it for myself. I didn't seem real to me when I heard Liam on the phone. When he said she had been killed, I was so certain there'd been a mistake..." Her breath shuddered as she looked at Sabrina's car. "This is all my fault."

"Do you have any idea what might've happened?" Bethany asked, her brows drawing together as she tried to make sense of Ellie's comment.

"No, nothing like that. I'm the one who sent her to deliver these pizzas. If we had been even a few minutes slower or faster at getting the pizzas packed up, none of this would have happened."

"Then it might have happened to someone else," the other woman said. "You can't blame yourself for these events. The blame rests solely on the shoulders of whoever hit her, if that's what happened." She patted Ellie's arm.

"Now, I should get back to work. I have to question some of the residents, just in case any of them heard or saw something. You just sit tight, okay? It won't be long until Russell's here."

Ellie nodded, feeling numb. She watched the young deputy walk away, then slid back into the driver's seat of her car, not bothering to turn the heat on. Her eyes were glued Sabrina's empty vehicle. Despite Bethany's words, she couldn't help but blame herself. Sabrina's death would be a shock to everyone at the pizzeria. Even though she had only worked there for a short time, Sabrina had been one of their own.

She had to wait only a few minutes before Russell's truck pulled to a stop behind her car. He hurried over to her window. She saw relief wash across his face when he saw her. She got out and he pulled her into a hug.

"I know Liam said it was one of your employees, but when I saw your car here…" He shook his head. "I'm glad you're okay. What are you doing here?"

"I don't know," Ellie said. "I just felt like I had to come and see it, after Liam told me what happened. I don't know what I was expecting. I hoped that he was wrong, I suppose. Russell, how could this have happened? They said that someone attacked her."

After she spoke, she realized that they had never actually said that. They had said that Sabrina had died from an injury to the head, and she had made the leap to an attack herself. She supposed it could have been an accident. Had she slipped and fallen? Hit her head on the unforgiving asphalt?

She shook herself. "Well, they don't know what happened yet. I just can't believe it, Russell. An hour ago, we were at the pizzeria together. She was tired; she had been driving all day. When I heard that there had been a car accident – which is what Liam thought at first – I thought it was my fault for not making her take a break. But now, knowing that someone might have attacked her, someone might have done this to her on purpose, it's not any better. How could anyone do this?"

"I don't know," the sheriff replied. "I promise, I'll get to the bottom of this. Whoever killed Sabrina won't get away with it."

"Hey, Russ!" Liam had noticed that his boss was on the scene, and was waving him over. Russell leaned down and gave Ellie a quick kiss.

"I've got to go," he said. "Go handle things at the pizzeria. I'll see you later."

Ellie watched him go. She gazed at the scene for one more moment, then turned back to her car. Her head snapped back around, doing a double take. On the yard, nearest to where Sabrina's body had been found, there were two pizza boxes, their contents scattered. She frowned. If she remembered correctly, the order that Sabrina had been delivering had only been for one pizza, so why were there two boxes at the scene of the crime?

CHAPTER FIVE

"I'm sure all of you know why I called you in today," she began, looking at the four employees gathered in front of her. Two were missing; Clara, who had left a few weeks ago to work at another small restaurant in town, and, of course, Sabrina. "A member of our team was killed last night while she was out on a delivery."

None of her employees were surprised by this news. When she had gotten back to the pizzeria the night before, she had found Rose still waiting for her. After telling the young woman what had happened, she had sent out an email to the others, who by then had heard about Sabrina's death from Rose, and asked them to meet at the pizzeria early the next morning. It was obvious that the news had hit them hard; Iris's eyes were red-rimmed from crying, and all of them looked as if they hadn't slept at all. She didn't feel much better herself; she had tossed and turned all night, and had left the house that morning without her customary cup of coffee, not feeling able to stomach the bitter drink.

"I don't know much about what happened, yet," she said. "No one does. Today, I just wanted to talk about what we're going to do here at the pizzeria. I know she didn't work here long, but she was still one of us. I want to be sure we give her the respect she deserves."

"Are we going to open today?" Jacob asked. "That would feel weird, after what happened."

"I was thinking we'd keep the pizzeria closed for a couple of days," she replied. "We can stay closed today, tomorrow, and Sunday, and reopen on Monday. Does that sound okay with everyone?"

They nodded, all four of them much more somber than usual. Ellie closed her eyes, feeling a rush of emotion again for her missing employee.

"I don't know yet when her funeral or memorial service will be, but I think we should all go if we can. I'm just as lost about all of this as you are, but if anyone needs to talk about it, you can come to me."

"Should we, I don't know, do something for her parents or something?" Iris asked.

"I'm not sure," Ellie said. "I don't want to intrude. We didn't know her all that well."

"You don't have any idea who did it?" Pete asked.

"No," she replied. "We don't even know what happened yet. I don't want to say anything until the police know for sure. I don't want to spread any rumors about this that aren't true."

"I just can't believe it," Rose said. "When you told me she'd been in an accident, I just thought she was on her way to the hospital or something. I didn't think she was dead."

"I wish that were true," Ellie said. "I didn't really know what was going on myself at the time. Trust me, this is just as shocking and horrifying for me as it is for all of you. As her employer, I'm the one that was responsible for her well-being while she was working here. Regardless of what happened, it won't change the fact that she was out there delivering pizzas because I asked her to. We may have to put deliveries on hold until we figure out what happened. I don't want to take the chance of it happening again and someone else getting hurt."

"You don't think that whoever did this would do it again?" Jacob asked. "I'm sure it was just an accident – she was probably in the wrong place at the wrong time. No one's targeting pizza delivery drivers."

"I agree that sounds unlikely, but I don't want to take the chance," Ellie said again. "Something just doesn't feel right about this."

She didn't tell her employees about the second pizza box she had seen at the scene of Sabrina's death. She still wasn't sure what to think of it herself. After getting back to the pizzeria the evening before, she had gone over the receipts, and confirmed that there had indeed only been one pizza on that delivery. Why had there been two boxes in the yard? She had mentioned it to Russell, of course, and he had told her he would put it in his notes. Neither of them knew what to think. It was a mystery, and one that she wasn't anywhere near solving.

"Anyway, that's all I wanted to talk about today. Feel free to go home, or do whatever you want. We will resume normal shifts on Monday. Until then, just keep Sabrina in your thoughts. If I learn anything new, I'll share it with all of you, I promise."

She watched as her employees rose and filed out slowly. She knew it would take them all some time to come to terms with Sabrina's death, which was one of the reasons she was keeping the pizzeria closed. They were all human, and it wouldn't be fair to expect them to work through their grief.

It wasn't just her small team of employees that would still be reeling with the shock of Sabrina's death. Kittiport was a tightly knit community, and the death of such a young woman would have the entire town in an uproar. It was the perfect crime if someone had wanted to get everyone's attention. Ellie knew that the news would be following the investigation of Sabrina's death closely. The killer was sure to get his or her ten minutes of fame when he was caught. She just hoped that the person responsible was found sooner rather than later. Even though she didn't want to admit it to the others, she was worried about them. Back in Chicago, she had heard stories of delivery drivers being mugged, but never thought it could happen somewhere like Kittiport.

Had it been a mugging, though? She had yet to talk to Russell about the incident in depth, but surely he would have mentioned it to her if Sabrina's wallet or other personal possessions had been stolen. Besides, what would an opportunistic mugger be doing on Green Street? Kittiport was small enough that it didn't exactly have a bad side of town, but even if it did, Green Street would be far from it.

She shook her head, pushing the mystery aside for the time being. With nothing to work off of, and not a single clue to point her in the direction of what might have happened, she knew that she wouldn't get anywhere and she was frustrated with this line of thinking. With her employees gone, the pizzeria was silent and empty. It reminded her disturbingly of a morgue, which she supposed was fitting, considering what had happened.

Not wanting to spend more time than was necessary in the building, she grabbed her purse off the counter and walked out the door. She wanted to go home, and do what she could to begin sorting through her own feelings about her employee's death.

"Ms. Pacelli?"

She jumped at the sound of someone saying her name. *Sabrina's death really has me on edge,* she thought as she turned around to see Kyle standing near the edge of the building.

"Sorry, the front door was locked. You said to come back later to talk about a possible position over the holidays?"

She bit back a sigh. By later, she had meant in a few weeks, and definitely not the day after one of her employees had passed away. She realized he may not yet know about the incident, and she didn't have the energy to tell him.

"Sorry — Kyle, wasn't it? Now isn't a good time. Bring me a resume sometime next week and we can talk about it."

"What day would be best?"

"I don't know," she said, distracted. "Monday."

"Okay. Thanks. I'll see you then. Have a nice day."

"You too," she said, giving him a vague wave as she turned towards her car. All she wanted was to get home and try to sort out her feelings. Everything else would have to wait until later.

CHAPTER SIX

B eing home was comforting. With Bunny at her heels and the sound of Marlowe chatting away in her cage in the other room, Ellie knew that she wasn't alone. One problem with being engaged to the sheriff was that whenever something bad happened, he was inevitably busy with work. That meant that she didn't have his shoulder to cry on when she needed it the most. Of course, she still had her grandmother.

Nonna was in the kitchen, her usual spot when she wasn't watching television or taking a nap, or out with one of her many friends. The kitchen table looked out across the backyard, which ended at the edge of the state park. White pines – Maine's state tree – filled the view. Ellie had never been completely comfortable with the forest. It didn't help that she had been involved in a couple of frightening experiences in that forest. Even if nothing bad had ever happened in there, however, she would still be uncomfortable with the dark spaces between the trees, where anyone or anything could be hiding. If it was just her living alone in the house, she would have shut the curtains the second it started getting dark out, but her grandmother liked leaving the drapes open so she could look outside and admire the stars and occasional glimpses of visiting wildlife.

Right now, of course, the sun was shining and the forest looked much less intimidating than it did in the evenings. Ellie walked over to the stove and filled up the tea kettle, placing it on one of the burners. Her grandmother was reading the newspaper and sipping a mug of tea.

"Anything interesting in there?" she asked, taking her favorite mug out of the drying rack beside the sink. She regretted her words almost immediately. She knew that Sabrina's death was on the front page, and closed her eyes, hoping that her grandmother wouldn't bring it up.

"The last farmer's market of the season is this Sunday," her grandmother said, putting the paper down. "I'll miss the fresh veggies."

Ellie relaxed. She had mentioned her employee's death to her grandmother that morning, but hadn't mentioned any details about it, and was glad that the older woman seemed to realize she needed to think about something else for a while.

"Okay, we can go together," Ellie said. "Do you mind if I see if Shannon wants to join us?"

"No, of course not. I like her. Do you think Russell will come along as well? I haven't seen him for a while."

"I don't know," she replied. "He is going to be pretty busy with this case —" she broke off, angry at herself for approaching the very subject that she had wanted her grandmother to avoid.

"Of course." Her grandmother looked away from her face. "Ellie, just let me know when you're ready to talk about it, okay?"

Ellie nodded. "I will. Thanks, Nonna." She cleared her throat. "So, um, what you want to do for lunch today? The pizzeria's closed until Monday, so I won't be going into work at all today."

"Well, we have that chicken in the fridge that needs to be cooked. I was thinking of making a chicken pot pie later. It's good comfort food, and I think we have all of the ingredients."

"That sounds wonderful," she said. "Let me know if you need any help."

By the time she finished her tea, she was almost regretting closing the pizzeria for the day. She would've felt better at work in the kitchen, making herself useful and actually doing something instead of just moping around the house. She felt something nudge her leg. She looked down to see Bunny gazing up at her hopefully. *There's still someone who needs me*, she thought, giving the little dog a smile.

"Do you want to go outside?" she asked. Bunny gave a single bark, her universal signal for yes. "Okay. Just a short walk, all right?"

It felt good to be outside. It was chilly enough that she was wearing a light sweatshirt, but it felt good after the heat of the summer. She loved the salty scent of the oceanside air, and the sounds of the wind and the surf. The road she lived on was sparsely populated, and as she walked further away from her house and the town, the houses got further and further apart until she was alone with nothing but the road, the trees, and to her right, the coast.

Bunny was familiar with their walks, and knew exactly where they were going. She sniffed along the edge of the road as they walked, happy as could be. The little papillon had been with Ellie for the past three years, and was her constant companion. Ellie loved the little dog, and was glad to see that she didn't seem to be suffering at all from her broken leg that she had endured not too long ago. Her small bones may be fragile, but they healed fast.

"It really is beautiful out here, huh?" she said as they walked. Even though she knew that the dog couldn't understand her, the way Bunny's little tail started to wag faster felt like an agreement to her.

She and the dog moved off the road to make room for a car that sped past. It reminded her that she wasn't all alone out here; she was surrounded by people, even if she couldn't see them. There were houses back in the trees, cars zipping by, and people out on the water in boats. There were people all around... and one of them was a killer.

The thought made her shiver. She decided to call Russell when she got home. She needed to ask him about what had happened. Even if he couldn't say anything officially, he might have some ideas. She hated not knowing. Were her other employees in danger? Was she in danger? Was anyone in town safe anymore?

She had faith that Russell would find whoever had killed her employee, but that didn't mean that she wanted to just sit back and wait while he did all of the leg work. She had known Sabrina personally so this wasn't something that she could just sit back and let someone else handle.

"All right, girl, it's time to head back," she said. Her ears were getting chilled since she hadn't brought a hat, and she wanted to call her fiancé sooner rather than later.

When she got in, she brought Marlowe with her to her home office. She placed the big red parrot on the wooden perch by the office window and took a seat at the desk. It was her grandfather's office; a large room with sturdy furniture and bookshelves lining the walls. She had redone some of it, replacing the chair with something more modern and comfortable and updating the electronics in the room, but it still reminded her of Arthur Pacelli, which was odd since she had barely known the man. She supposed she must have had a few old memories of being in the room when she was a child. She felt a pang of regret for the man that had impacted her life so much, but who she had never really taken the chance to get to know. There were some things that she would never be able to go back and fix, just like Sabrina's death. She may not be able to fix it, but she might be able to get the young woman some justice.

Just as she was reaching for her phone, it rang. She hesitated when she saw that it was Linda. The second pizzeria hadn't even crossed her mind once since Sabrina had been killed. Her hand hovered over the phone for a moment, then she pressed the red button to decline the call. She could deal with it later. Right now, she just wanted to talk to Russell.

She was glad when he answered the call. She knew he was probably busy, and resolved not to make the call too long. She didn't want to take any time away from him tracking down Sabrina's killer. She just had to know what he had discovered so far.

"Hey," she said. "How are you?"

"Tired," he admitted. "I was up all night working."

"On Sabrina's case?"

"Yeah," he said. "It's being investigated as a homicide right now."

"What happened? What did you find?"

"Well, forensics determined that she died from a blow to her temple. The weapon wasn't found at the scene. Someone attacked her, then fled."

"Was it a mugging?" she asked

"That's the thing. No. She had cash in her wallet, none of her cards seemed to be missing, and she was wearing jewelry when she was found."

"That's so odd," Ellie said. "You don't have any idea why they did it? Why someone killed her?"

"No. That makes it a lot harder. No motive makes it difficult to find a killer unless they left behind some sort of physical evidence. Fingerprints alone won't work unless they're already in the system."

"Do you think it was someone she knew? Were they targeting her, or was it just chance that she happened to be there?"

"There's no way to tell," he said. "Right now, I'm just going through the photos from the crime scene and reviewing all of the testimonies we have from the residents of the street."

"What about the second pizza box?" she asked. "Have you figured out what it was doing there?"

"No," he said. "That's the oddest thing about all of this. Are you sure that the order was only for one pizza?"

"Yes," she said. "I double checked the receipt when I got back."

"Well, it was definitely a Papa Pacelli's box. I'm really not sure what to think of it. I don't know if it has anything to do with the murder, or if it's just something odd. Maybe she accidentally grabbed a second pizza when she left the restaurant."

"Maybe," Ellie said doubtfully.

"I know this is hard you," he said. "I'm doing everything I can to get to the bottom of it."

"I know," she said "I —"

Her phone beeped, letting her know she had an incoming call. It was Shannon.

"Do you have to go?" her fiancé asked.

"It's your sister-in-law," she said. "I should probably take it. I'm sure she'll want to talk about all of this, I haven't spoken to her since it happened."

"Okay. I'll try to call you this evening when I get home. I'll let you know if I learn anything new," he said. "I love you."

"I love you too," she said. "Good luck. I hope you find something solid soon."

"Me too."

CHAPTER SEVEN

"**D**o you think I made the right decision?" she asked. "If it's what you want to do, then yes," Shannon said. "I think it's a very kind gesture."

"Thank you for putting me in contact with them. I wouldn't have known how to do it myself."

"I don't usually use my contacts from the paper for personal reasons, but I figured with everything they've been going through, they would appreciate the help."

"It's the least I could do. I feel so bad about —"

"Ellie." Shannon grabbed her by the arm and turned her around. "Stop blaming yourself. What happened isn't your fault at all. You had no way to know what was going to happen to her."

"But if I hadn't sent her —"

"Then it would have been Jacob, or Rose, Iris, or Pete, or some random late-night jogger that got attacked. James told me that Russell said that there's no reason to think that whoever did this was targeting Sabrina, which means that it was just plain chance that she was there. If it wasn't her, it would have been someone else."

Ellie sighed. "I know you're right, at least in my mind, but I still feel like I could have done something differently. I just feel so guilty about all of this."

"I know." Her friend gave her a sad smile. "It's a terrible situation all the way around. I usually love my job, but interviewing a couple of bereaved parents because my boss wants to run a news story on their deceased daughter, isn't exactly my idea of a great time either. The whole town is shocked by this, you know."

"I know. Everyone is going to be eager for the killer to get caught. Hopefully that will make things harder for whoever it is to hide. I hate the fact that while Sabrina's dead, the person who killed her is out there living their life like normal."

"That's what Russell's here for," Shannon said. "He'll do his job, don't worry."

She patted Ellie on the arm, then turned and pulled open the door to the community center. Inside, Ellie saw two people a little bit older than her who were talking to an official looking man in a suit. When she and Shannon came in, all three of them looked around. Shannon waved and headed towards them, with Ellie following behind her.

"Hi, Mr. and Mrs. Williams," Shannon said. "This is the woman I was telling you about, Eleanora Pacelli. She goes by Ellie."

"Hello, Ellie," the woman said. "When Shannon told us about your generous offer, I was so grateful. My name is Georgia. Georgia Williams. This is my husband, Manny. It's so nice to meet you."

Ellie shook hands with the woman, unprepared for how similar she looked to Sabrina. She looked just like the young woman, but aged thirty years. She felt a pang as she realized that Sabrina would never get to that age.

"I'm so sorry about your daughter," she said.

The other woman took a deep breath. "It still doesn't feel real," she said. "There are these moments where I forget that she's gone, and when I remember it's like finding out all over again…" Without warning, she began to sob. Her husband took her into his arms, and Ellie looked away, embarrassed. She shouldn't have mentioned anything. These people had just lost their daughter; of course they would be fragile.

"Like I said, Mr. and Mrs. Williams, there's no rush," the other man said. He turned Ellie. "I'm Dan Asado. I'm in charge of renting out the community center. I think we met before."

"I'm sure we have," the pizzeria owner replied. "I helped out during that snowstorm earlier this year."

He nodded. "I'm sure we've seen each other around. This was a nice offer for you to make. Like I told them, we'll do anything they need to make their daughter's memorial perfect."

"I think we should get going," Manny said. "I made you a list of some of her favorite things… her favorite colors, music, that sort of stuff. There are also some photos of her in this folder. We just want a nice, simple, memorial, something that she would appreciate if she were here to see it." He closed his eyes. "I can't believe I'm talking about this," he said through gritted teeth. "My baby girl –"

He broke off and now it was his wife's turned to comfort him. Ellie turned away, not wanting to intrude on their grief. She couldn't even begin to imagine what they were going through, and it brought a lump to her throat. None of this was fair. Sabrina had had her whole life in front of her, and no one had the right to take that away.

"Thank you," Georgia said again. "You don't know what this means to us. Having her gone is bad enough, but planning her memorial, I don't know if I could have done it alone."

Ellie turned back to her. "Don't worry, Mrs. Williams. I'll take care of everything I can. The team at the pizzeria will help too. Sabrina was a special girl, and we all miss her. You and your husband just worry about taking care of yourselves."

She watched as the couple left the building, leaning on each other for support. She was glad that she had made the offer to pay for Sabrina's memorial, and help her family however she could. At least she felt like she was doing *something*.

Dan cleared his throat. "So, it sounds like they've settled on the main room as the space for the memorial. I told them I'd waive the normal rental fee, considering the, er, the circumstances. However, we don't handle catering or decorations, so that will still have to be paid for…"

"I'll handle it," Ellie said. "Thank you. It's good to see the town pulling together for her."

"It's the least we could do. A tragedy like this…" He shook his head. "It never should have happened."

After leaving their short meeting with Sabrina's parents, Ellie and Shannon went out for lunch. It was a clear day, too nice to spend inside, so they grabbed a pair of sandwiches from the little shop by the marina and strolled along the docks until they reached the *Eleanora*, the Pacelli family's boat. The two of them set their sandwiches and soda on the table in the cabin, and settled down for a nice oceanside lunch together.

"I bet the waves are pretty strong out there today," Shannon said. "I even saw some whitecaps further out in the harbor."

"It would be a fun day to go out," Ellie said. "Too bad James and Russell are both busy working."

"Yeah." Her friend sighed. "I wouldn't be comfortable taking the boat out on rough seas myself. I can putter around the harbor, but I don't want to test my luck."

"I don't even know if I would be able to get it out of the marina without bumping into another boat," Ellie said. "I keep meaning to have Russell teach me how to navigate on the water, but I always forget whenever we're actually out here."

"Maybe next summer we can practice more," her friend said. "It would be nice to be able to go out just the two of us." Shannon frowned and placed a hand over her abdomen. "Well, it wouldn't be just the two of us, would it? I almost forgot about this little guy. I can still hardly believe it."

"How's James doing with it?"

"He's thrilled," Shannon said with a grin. "He's wanted kids forever. We tried for a long time, and gave up years ago. This really is a miracle. It's just also a shock. I was ready for a baby ten years ago. It's the last thing I expected to happen now. Don't get me wrong — it's a good thing. I'm excited. Just... also terrified."

Ellie wondered if her friend had spoken to her husband about all of this. "You know I'm here for you, right?" she said. "If you ever need anything, I'll do what I can to help."

"I know," Shannon said. "That's one reason James and I decided to stay in town. It may be a small community, but it *is* a community, which I love. We have you and Russell, and all of our other friends, and, well, you've seen how much the town has come together for Sabrina's death. I want my son or daughter to grow up in that sort of community. Yes, there are downsides to growing up in such a small town, but I think the positives outweigh the negatives."

"I'm glad you're staying," Ellie said. "This place wouldn't be the same without you."

The two women smiled at each other, then Shannon's eyes went wide. "Oh! I almost forgot. I found something odd the other day. One of the other ladies at the paper had a business card on her desk. It said it was for Papa Pacelli's, but the number was wrong, and it didn't have the store's email or website on it. It was really weird. I think I have it in here somewhere…" She pulled her purse onto the table and began digging through it. "Dang it, I must have left it at home."

Ellie frowned. "A Papa Pacelli's business card? I don't understand."

"It looked just like the cards you have at the pizzeria, but the contact info didn't match up," her friend said. "Maybe it was just an old card? Did you guys change your phone number recently?"

"No," the pizzeria owner said. "We didn't even have business cards until I took over, and we're still on the first printing, so it can't have been an old card. Something weird is definitely going on." She told her friend about the second pizza box she had seen at the scene of Sabrina's murder.

"That's odd," Shannon said. "Do you think there's someone out there poaching your business?"

"Maybe. I think I need to tell Russell about the card. Sorry to cut our lunch short, but it's going to bother me. Maybe he will have some ideas about what's going on."

"Let me know if the two of you come up with anything," her friend replied. "I'll keep an eye out for that card, and if I see anything suspicious, you'll be the first one to know."

CHAPTER EIGHT

"What is a cauliflower and parmesan crust pizza?"

"It's a low-carb pizza crust," Ellie said. She had been answering the question all day, but the reviews from those who tried the pizza were positive. "It's made with cauliflower, cheese, eggs, and a few spices. You can order it with any combination of toppings you would like."

"How is it different than your gluten free crust?" the customer asked.

"The gluten free crust is made with rice flour, which still has carbs in it," Ellie said. "The cauliflower crust is friendlier to people on a low-carb diet or those that have diabetes and have to watch their blood sugar."

"Does it still taste like a normal pizza?"

"It takes a little bit different, but it's still quite good. If you want to try it and you don't like it, we can offer you a full refund."

"Well… okay," woman said. "I always like to try new specials, so I suppose I'll give this one a try too. Can I get it with cheddar, mozzarella, mushrooms, peppers, and onions on it?"

"Sure thing. What size would you like?"

"I'll just take the medium, thanks," the woman said. "I'll tell my daughter about it too. She's trying that low-carb diet, and I'm sure it will make her happy to know that she can still eat pizza."

"Definitely," Ellie replied with a grin. "This is a test run to see how people like it, but if it's popular, we will keep offering it. I enjoy being able to offer people healthy choices, even at a little pizza joint like this. There's no reason that good food has to be synonymous with unhealthy food."

It felt good to be back at work, even though she was still mourning Sabrina's passing. It was the first time that the restaurant had been open since her death, and it was busier than ever. She wasn't comfortable with the idea of the pizzeria benefiting from her employee's death, but at the same time she knew that the townspeople meant well. They were here to show their support, and that meant a lot to her.

Armed with the new order, she went into the kitchen. It was time for her and Rose to switch places anyway, and she enjoyed making the new cauliflower pizza crusts. It was a major step away from her grandfather's old recipe, but she knew that it would never place the good old-fashioned pizza that everyone loved. She had tried the recipe at home the evening before, and had fallen in love with it. It was a great, healthy alternative to a regular pizza that would hopefully enable people to eat at the restaurant while still making healthy choices if they were on a diet or had medical needs.

One problem with the pizza was that they had to start fresh every day. With the normal pizza crusts, she usually pre-made them on the slower days, and let them chill in the fridge until they were needed. They couldn't do the same with the cauliflower crust, not with the raw eggs in the mix.

Not that it was that much work. Once the cauliflower had been run through a food processor, cooked, and left to chill for a couple of hours, it was simple enough to mix it up with the cheese, eggs, and spices each time someone ordered the crust. She had pre-processed a couple of heads of cauliflower that morning, and they were ready to go.

She took one of the pre-measured bowls of shredded cauliflower out of the fridge and brought it over to the crust making station in the kitchen. She cracked a couple of eggs, measured the scoops of cheese, and tossed in the seasoning before stirring the mixture with a wooden spoon. Once it was ready, she dumped it onto a baking sheet that had been lined with parchment paper and pressed it into the shape of a pizza crust. She put the pan into the oven so it could begin cooking, then got the other ingredients for the veggie pizza out of the refrigerator. When the timer dinged, she pulled the lightly browned cauliflower crust out of the oven and spread the sauce, cheese, and veggies over top of it. She put it back in the oven for another few minutes while the toppings cooked, washed her hands, and started folding up the box. It was a little bit more involved than making regular pizza, but it really didn't take much once she got the hang of it.

A few minutes later, she returned to the front with the woman's pizza box. She handed it over with a smile, then returned to the kitchen to begin work on the next couple of orders. She was surprised when a little bit later, someone walked through the door to the kitchen – and it wasn't one of her employees. It was the young man that had been interested in working at the pizzeria, Kyle.

"Shoot," she muttered. She'd completely forgotten that she had promised to see him on Monday.

"Sorry, is it a bad time?" he asked. "Rose sent me back here."

"No," she said. "It's fine as long as you don't mind doing the interview while I'm working."

"Not at all," he said. "What should I do to help?"

"Oh, nothing," she said. "Take a seat if you'd like. Let me finish washing the dishes, then we can get started."

Feeling frazzled, she joined him at the table a couple of minutes later. He had a folder in front of him, and was wearing a button up shirt and slacks. He had certainly dressed for the interview. She forced herself to smile and tried to relax. It wasn't his fault that he had interrupted her at a busy time. She had told him to come in anytime on Monday, and couldn't be upset that he had taken her up on the offer.

"So, why are you interested in working here?" she asked.

"Well, I eat here a lot," he said, chuckling. "No, the truth is, I've always been interested in working in a restaurant. Most places require experience prior to hiring you, at least if you want to work with food, which, I'll be honest, I don't have. I mean, I cook a lot at home, but I haven't ever been paid to work in the kitchen before."

"So, you'd be interested primarily in a kitchen position?" she asked. The truth was that they needed another delivery driver – Jacob had been interested in driving less and spending more time working in the restaurant itself, and Pete couldn't handle all the deliveries on his own. Rose and Iris could do deliveries occasionally, but their vehicles weren't really well-suited to the amount of driving around that a dedicated delivery driver would need to do. However, she didn't want to overlook Kyle if he was serious about his passion for cooking. They would be able to make do, and could hire another employee in a couple of months if they were still having issues with getting all of the deliveries done.

"Yes, though I can start in delivery or something if that's what you need right now," he said, as if he had read her mind. "I'm hoping to get experience in a kitchen and maybe one day open my own restaurant." He backpedaled quickly. "I don't mean I want to compete directly with you guys. No, I'd go to another town and open it there."

"Relax," she said, chuckling. "I don't mind if you do want to open a restaurant here in Kittiport. I'm not afraid of a little competition. Of course, if you work here, you will learn some of our secret recipes. My grandfather's crust recipe, especially, is important to me. I would ask that you don't use it if you do end up opening your own restaurant down the road."

"Of course not," he said. "If you want me to sign something or…"

"We can talk about that later. Right now, why don't you tell me a little bit about yourself."

"Here's my resume, and I also printed off a cover letter." He chuckled. "Sorry. My dad is in business himself, and he always tells me that it's better to be too formal than too casual."

"Thanks," she said, taking the folder. "I'll look at it later. Right now, just tell me about who you are. How long have you lived in Kittiport?" If he was going to be doing any deliveries, he would need to know the town pretty well.

"Well, I moved here with my parents three years ago, and finished up my last year of high school here. I've been taking college classes online. It's easier that way and my mom, well, she has some health issues and needs help sometimes. My dad travels a lot. You probably don't want to hear about my family's life, though. I've been working at that gas station on the road between here and Benton Harbor since I graduated. My manager is pretty cool, and I would be leaving on good terms with everyone there. I just want to start doing something that is more relevant to the career I want, if that makes sense. I want to be creative, and not just work behind a counter for my whole life."

"It does," Ellie said. "Now, as you know, we lost one of our employees recently. I don't think I'm ready to make a new hire quite yet, but what I'll do is I'll take a look at your resume and if everything checks out, you'll be the first on the list when I am ready. Does that sound okay? I'm sorry that you won't have an answer right away, and I understand if you find something else in the meantime."

"I'm willing to wait," he said. "Thank you for considering me, Ms. Pacelli. It means a lot."

He rose and shook her hand before leaving. Ellie looked at the folder he had left behind, feeling too tired and sad to go through it just then. She stood up and tucked it away in a drawer, getting back to work. The pizzas wouldn't cook themselves.

CHAPTER NINE

" Just a little over to the right," Ellie said. "Perfect."

She stepped back to admire the soft glow of the white lights. The effect was beautiful. She had seen the community center dressed up for quite a few different occasions, but Sabrina's memorial had to be the most significant. She was glad that she was able to be involved in it. Yes, it was more work, but it was worth it. The more she thought about everything that was going on, the more she was sure the crime was somehow connected to the pizzeria. With the mysterious business card floating around and the second pizza box as the crime scene, she was certain that there was something going on that none of them were yet aware of.

Shannon still hadn't been able to find the business card. Ellie didn't blame her – with her pregnancy, she had a lot of her own things going on. Ellie had kept her eyes out for anything suspicious over the past few days, but hadn't noticed anything. Other than the lingering mystery of the young woman's death, things were slowly returning to normal in the town. She knew this memorial would be cathartic for all of them.

Her employees had been handling most of the decorations. Rose, Iris, Pete, and Jacob were happy to spend their Sunday morning putting up lights, setting up the table of photos and memorabilia from Sabrina's life, and putting together the playlist for the coming afternoon. She was handling the catering. Not pizza – she thought that the memorial called for something a little bit more refined. She had contacted the White Pine Kitchen, and they were supplying catering for a steep discount in honor of Sabrina.

Everything was going smoothly, and the memorial was set to start in just a couple of hours. She knew that most of the town would come through the doors before the event was over. She hoped that the experience wouldn't be too painful for Sabrina's parents. She hadn't heard from them since the meeting the week before.

"Oh, Ellie, it's wonderful," Shannon said, walking over to stand next to her. "James will be here in a little bit. Is Russell coming?"

"Yes," Ellie said. "He's going to be here for the last half of the memorial."

"Are you going to be here for the whole thing?"

"I feel like I should stay," she replied. "I told her parents I would handle everything, and part of that means being here. I don't know how long they will be able to stay for. This is going to be pretty hard on them."

Her friend nodded. "Of course. Well, James and I will stay until Russell shows up. I wasn't feeling well this morning, but it seems to have passed – for now. The joys of pregnancy." She chuckled.

Ellie gave her a small smile. "You're in for an adventure," she said. "I can't really say I envy you, at least not this part. Morning sickness sounds like something that I would not want to deal with."

"I just have to keep reminding myself it's temporary," she said. "Supposedly it goes away later in the pregnancy."

"Sorry I don't have any sage advice to offer you," she said. "I–"

"Hi Ms. P.," someone said. Fighting back annoyance at the interruption, Ellie turned around to see Sadie standing behind her. She smiled at the young woman, reminding herself that this was Sabrina's best friend. She must have been hurting. "Hi Sadie, can I do anything for you?"

"I was actually going to ask you that," she said. "What can I do to help?"

"How about you go help Iris with the flowers? People sent a lot of them to her parents, and they dropped them off here this morning so we could set them up around the memorial. There are a couple of extra tables in the storage area if you need any more space."

"I'll do that, thanks."

Ellie watched the young woman walk away. Shannon shook her head.

"Man, I keep forgetting just how many lives poor Sabrina's death impacted. Her parents, everyone at work, everyone that she went school with, her best friend... Her killer is the most hated person in Kittiport. Hopefully Russell finds them soon. If the suspect's name gets slipped before he's arrested, a riot just might break out as this town hunts him down."

"I don't think there's any danger of that," Ellie said with a sigh. "They still have no idea who it is. They can't find anyone who would have had a motive to kill her. Nothing was stolen, she hasn't had any recent breakups – she didn't even have a boyfriend. I just keep thinking of that second pizza box that shouldn't have been there. That's the only thing that was out of place at the crime scene, but Russell still hasn't found out anything about it."

It was frustrating, even though she knew that these things took time and everyone was working as hard as they could on the case. If only Shannon had been able to locate the business card, they might be able to get to the bottom of this.

The memorial went smoothly. Sabrina's parents thanked her profusely when they got there. Ellie spent most of her time standing on the sidelines, not wanting to intrude too much. People came and went, paying their respects to the memory of the girl who had died too early. Ellie was relieved when Russell arrived. He sought her out, and stayed by her side for the rest of the afternoon. She was glad to have him there. The day had made her feel emotional, and she didn't want to be alone.

As it was beginning to wind down, he invited her over to his house for the rest of the evening. She was glad to accept. They had a lot to talk about. Hopefully between the two of them, they would be able to crack the mystery of Sabrina's death.

CHAPTER TEN

It was good to be at Russell's house after the busy day. She had spent the last few hours constantly surrounded by people, and the peace and quiet was soothing.

Grabbing a can of diet soda from his fridge, she sat on the couch and leaned into the soft cushions, enjoying having the freedom to relax at last. "Thanks for coming," she said.

"Of course. Even if you hadn't been so involved in the memorial, I would have made an appearance. Sabrina's death has affected the entire town," he said. "Being there did make it all the more frustrating that I've been unable to crack this case. I want so badly to be able to give her parents the closure that they need, but without physical evidence or even a motive, what can I do?"

"What have you found out about the pizza boxes and the business card I told you about?"

"It seems to be a dead end," he said. "If we had the business card, I could track down the person who owns the phone number on it, but without it, I don't know what I can do."

"What about the pizza box?" she asked.

"What about it?" He gave a dry laugh. "It's just a box from your restaurant, like any other. It's weird, but it's not going to send anybody to prison on its own. Sorry, I'm just getting fed up with this whole case. I hate that I'm so powerless."

"Can't you, I don't know, dust it for fingerprints or something?"

"I tried that," he said, shaking his head. "First of all, cardboard isn't exactly ideal for taking prints anyway. There were a couple of oil smudges that held good quality prints, but nothing that raised any alarms. Even if I found prints that weren't from anyone at the pizzeria, unless they were already in the system, it wouldn't help."

"Do you think whoever did this is an experienced killer?" she asked, giving voice to something that had been worrying her. With the lack of evidence, she was frightened that this was someone who was used to killing and getting away with it.

"Honestly, no," he said. "I think it was something that happened in the heat of the moment. I don't think it was premeditated at all.

87

Whoever did this wasn't hiding in a dark alley waiting for his next victim to come along. He was on Green Street at nine at night – it's not exactly the ideal place for a would-be killer to lurk. I do think that the killer must have been someone she knew, and he or she *must* have had a motive. And unless they had access to the list of deliveries, they would only have come upon her by chance. I already cleared your employees, so since they were the only ones that would have been able to see the deliveries scheduled for that night, I'm leaning towards the encounter being happenstance."

"You suspected that one of my employees may have been the killer?" she asked, upset even though she didn't know why.

"I asked them all for alibis," he said. "While I don't think any of them did it, it wouldn't make sense to ignore them as possible suspects. You know as well as I do that most homicides are committed by someone the person knows. It makes sense to check out the people she was working with."

Ellie nodded. It hadn't even crossed her mind that the killer might be someone that worked at the pizzeria. She trusted them all.

"Hey," he said, sitting down next to her. "We'll find this person. I know it's taking longer than we wanted, but something's bound to come up."

"If only we could find out what they wanted," she said. "Why would anyone want to kill Sabrina?"

"Well, we've already gone over all the possible motives I could think of, but maybe we should go over them again. We know she didn't have a boyfriend," he said. "There's nothing on her social media pages about it, nothing in her phone records that would indicate that she was seeing someone secretly, and her parents confirmed that she wasn't seeing anyone, as did her best friend. She hadn't had any recent breakups, either. I would say that love probably isn't the motive here, unless she was seeing someone whom she was keeping very secret."

"Okay, so this wasn't a lover's quarrel," Ellie said. "What else? It wasn't money; whoever killed her didn't take the cash out of her wallet, they didn't steal her credit cards, and they didn't take her jewelry."

"It wasn't money or love," Russell said. "How about jealousy?"

"Well, she had a good relationship with her parents, a job at the pizzeria, she was pretty, she was all set to get her bachelor's degree in a couple of years... so maybe."

"Next we would have to determine how killing her would benefit the suspect. Either he was acting out of anger, or he was hoping to manipulate things with her death to get something out of it. Who would benefit from her death?"

Russell was gazing off into the distance now, working through the problem in his own mind. Ellie didn't bother answering him. Instead, she thought about what he had said. Who would benefit from her death? If they didn't stand to gain love or money, what would they gain?

Russell's previous words came back to her. Sabrina had a job. A job that someone Ellie knew wanted very badly. She frowned. Kyle didn't seem like the killing type. And who would kill for a pizza job? Yes, she could give him the experience in a working kitchen that he needed to jumpstart his career as a chef, but there were a couple of other restaurants around town that would likely be willing to do the same thing for him. She knew that Joanna would be hiring new employees eventually, and while heating up hot dogs wasn't exactly the same thing as making a pizza from scratch, it would at least give him something cooking related to put on his resume. There is also the Lobster Pot, and the White Pine Kitchen, both of which would likely let him start as a dishwasher and work his way up. It was hard to see a spot in her kitchen as being motive for murder, but now that it had occurred to her, she couldn't keep silent about it.

"Russell, there is this kid who has been interested in working for me," she began. "He stopped by a couple of days before Sabrina died. I told him at the time that we weren't hiring just then. He stopped in again while I was at the pizzeria on Friday talking to the employees. I told him to come on Monday, with a resume and I'd take a look at it, and he did. He seems very interested in the job, and now that Sabrina's gone, we obviously have a spot. Do you think that he could have done it?"

"I suppose he could have," Russell said, frowning. "Did he know her?"

"I don't think so, but it's a small town. What I don't understand is how he would know that she would be there on Green Street at that specific house, at that specific time."

"Maybe he didn't. Like I said, it seems like it was the impromptu decision. Could you do me a favor and get me his contact information?"

"Of course."

"Thank you." He leaned over and kissed her. "Do you want to take a walk? I've been inside all day, I'd like to get some fresh air before it gets too cold this evening."

As they set off down the sidewalk a few minutes later, Ellie was struck by a memory, something she had almost forgotten. The last time she and Russell had walked down this street she had seen the mysterious late-night pizza delivery car. At the time, she had thought it belonged to a pizzeria from another town that had decided to begin encroaching on Papa Pacelli's territory, but now she wasn't so sure. Those three things – the pizza delivery car that was where it shouldn't have been, the second pizza box, and the mysterious business card Shannon had found – they all pointed towards a bigger mystery. The only question was, what was it?

CHAPTER ELEVEN

The first thing she did when she got to the pizzeria the next day was to open Kyle's folder, which contained his resume and cover letter. She had yet to look at it, now that she took the time, she saw something that made her breath catch. Kyle's address. He lived on Green Street.

She took a photo of the file and emailed it to Russell, then called to let him know what she had done. "I can't believe I didn't realize this sooner," she said. "If only I had looked at his resume when he first gave it to me, I would have seen it. It's him, it has to be. I can't believe I interviewed him, was even considering hiring him, and all along he was her killer." She was disgusted. She had spent so much time hating Sabrina's killer, but when she had come face-to-face with him, she hadn't recognized him.

"I'll bring him in for questioning," he said. "I'm on my way out the door right now. I'll let you know what happens."

She shoved her phone in her pocket and stared at the folder. She was in shock. She knew that she should be glad that they had likely just solved Sabrina's murder, but she was so horrified with herself for not noticing sooner. It seemed obvious now. Kyle had a motive for murder, and he would be easy to place near the scene at the right time.

Wondering if his cover letter would tell her anything about what sort of person he was, she began to read it, but found nothing to satisfy her. He seemed like a normal young man. It made her skin crawl. How could someone capable of taking a young woman's life seem so normal on paper?

"Hey, Ms. P.."

She jumped. Jacob had come in without her noticing. Quickly, she shoved the paper back into the folder. "Hey, Jacob," she said. "How are you?"

"Not too bad," he said. He glanced at the folder, but evidently decided not to ask about her strange reaction. She was glad. She didn't want to tell him what was going on, on the off chance that she and Russell were wrong. She didn't want Shannon's words at the memorial to come back to haunt her. It would be terrible to start a town-wide manhunt on someone innocent. "Thanks for asking. So, what's the menu for today?"

"We're still serving the cauliflower crust pizza," she said. "Sorry, but I've been so distracted by everything with Sabrina that I haven't set up anything for this week's special. I'll get around to it tomorrow."

"That's fine, people seem to like the cauliflower crust anyway," he said. "We don't exactly have a lot of health food options in this town."

She smiled. "No, that's true." She remembered with a pang that there would be no more farmer's markets until next year. She had enjoyed visiting the last one with her grandmother, even though the pickings had been a bit slim. The season was gradually changing, and soon enough they would be facing the end of another year.

She realized that she hadn't thought about the second pizzeria very much over the past week. Linda had been forced to deal with some of the issues that had arisen on her own, and Ellie was pleasantly surprised to see that she had managed it quite well. The time for the grand opening was drawing nearer and nearer. She was less nervous than she had been before. Somehow, Sabrina's death had reminded her that her own problems, while important to her, weren't very important in the grand scheme of things. Even if the second pizzeria ended up being a complete disaster, she would still have her family and her friends by her side, and the rest of her life to branch out and achieve her goals.

"So, do you want me to drive delivery today?"

She blinked, drawn back to the present by Jacob's question. They hadn't accepted any delivery orders for the past week, while she had been figuring out what Sabrina's murder meant for the pizzeria. *I guess we can start doing them again,* she thought. *Russell's about to arrest the person responsible, so no one will be in danger any longer.*

"If you're comfortable doing it," she said.

"I am. I'll just keep my eyes open and be careful. If someone's out there, they're probably less likely to attack a guy than a girl. Pete and I should probably be the only ones to do deliveries for a while."

"That's very gallant of you," she said, smiling. "I'd better go start opening for the day. If you could pre-heat the ovens and restock the soda fridge out front, that would be great."

"Will do," he said.

She got to work, turning on the lights in the dining area and flipping the sign from closed to open before unlocking the door. She kept her phone with her, hoping Russell would tell her as soon as Kyle was found. She wanted closure, and she was sure Sabrina's parents did too. The whole town would be able to rest easier at night knowing that the killer was apprehended and safely locked away.

However, the call that she was waiting for didn't come. She checked her phone every time she got a break, but Russell hadn't called or texted her. That meant only one thing; that he hadn't found Kyle yet. Had she waited too long? What if Kyle had gotten nervous and left town? She hoped that wasn't the case. For Sabrina, as well as everyone else in town, she wanted him to face justice for what he did.

She stayed late at the pizzeria, cleaning and scrubbing, letting all of her anxieties melt away in the best way she knew how. The kitchen was sparkling by the time she was done. She didn't feel much better, but at least she had killed an extra hour. It was time to go home, call Russell, and see what was going on.

She grabbed the pair of black garbage bags that held the day's trash and stepped out through the employee entrance in the back to take them to the dumpster. She froze halfway through the door. There was a shadowed form standing by the dumpster, digging through the bags inside. Her first thought was that one of her employees had dropped something inside, but something about the shape made her hesitate. The person was wearing a dark sweatshirt with the hood drawn up over their head. The movements were furtive and cautious, as if he was trying to finish what he was doing before anyone saw him. Someone who had a valid reason for being there wouldn't look like that. Ellie wanted to grab her phone, but to do so she would have to put down the garbage bags, and then the plastic would rustle and alert him to her presence. Instead, she stood frozen, watching as the person sorted through the garbage. To her surprise, what he pulled out was an empty pizza box.

"What are you doing?" she snapped. The person jumped. The pizza box in his hand went flying, and he turned to sprint down the road. Ellie was stunned. She had spoken without thinking first. She should have waited to see what the person in the hoodie did after that. Seeing the pizza box had reminded her of the whole mystery surrounding her employee's death, and she had forgotten the need for secrecy.

She dropped the bags and took a hesitant step forward, her mind racing. What was this person doing, stealing empty pizza boxes out of the dumpster? She began to connect the dots. The pizza delivery car late at night, the second pizza box where there should only have been one, the business card with the phone number on it that wasn't Papa Pacelli's... Someone was trying to steal business from her.

It seemed far-fetched, but the evidence was here in front of her eyes. What other reason could someone have for stealing empty pizza boxes if they weren't planning on using them?

She hesitated only a second before she took off running after the person. She had never been a fan of jogging, but she was relatively fit from her long walks with Bunny and Russell. That and the fact that she stayed on her feet all day at the pizzeria meant that she had more stamina than she thought. She wasn't gaining on the person, but she wasn't losing ground either. She saw the person make a sharp turn between two buildings. She ran after them, and found to her relief that they had stumbled right into a fence. The mysterious thief was trapped.

She reached forward and yanked the person's hood back, expecting to reveal Kyle. What she saw instead made her gasp.

"You?"

CHAPTER TWELVE

S adie stared back at her, her eyes wide. "I'm sorry," she said. "I didn't know that taking something out of a dumpster was a crime."

"It's not." Ellie realized she actually had no idea whether or not it was. "Well, at least that's not why I was chasing you. I thought you were someone else. I'm sorry."

Sadie frowned. "Who did you think I was?"

"Just this guy..." She sighed. Sadie had been Sabrina's best friend. She deserved to know. "Don't tell anyone, but we think we know who the killer is. There's this guy, Kyle, who has been wanting to work here, and something weird had been going on with the pizzeria, so when I saw someone going through the dumpster, everything just sort of came together and seemed to make sense. Obviously, I was wrong. Sorry again for frightening you."

"That's all right. Um, I should probably get going."

"Wait," Ellie said. "What *were* you doing?"

"I was just… looking for something." She shook her head. "It's not important. I really should be going."

Ellie frowned as the young woman inched around her.

"Wait. I want you to tell me, why are you taking empty pizza boxes?"

"I wasn't –"

"I think you should come with me," Ellie said, a new suspicion beginning to simmer inside of her. She didn't know exactly what was happening, but it was evident that Sadie had something to do with it.

Before the young woman could slip away, Ellie had grabbed her by her arm walking back down the road. Sadie followed reluctantly. Ellie marched to the employee entrance and tugged it open. Stepping past the garbage bags, she led Sadie inside. "Wait at the table," she said. "I'm going to call the sheriff."

"Ellie, sorry I didn't get back to you sooner," he said, not giving her a chance to speak when he first answered. "I haven't found Kyle yet. I got in touch with one of his friends from work and according to her, he's out of town for the next couple of days."

"That's all right," Ellie said. "That's not what I want to talk about anyway." She lowered her voice. "Sadie, that friend of Sabrina's, was digging through the dumpster outside the pizzeria when I went to take the trash out. She was pulling out empty pizza boxes, and when I confronted her she acted oddly. I think you should come here and talk to her."

"Hold on," he said. "Where is she now?"

"She's here. I brought her back to the pizzeria."

"I'll be right over," he said. "Just… be careful, alright?"

She set the phone down and turned to find Sadie getting out of her chair. "Where are you going?" she asked.

"I'm getting out of here," the young woman said.

"No, you need to stay. Russell is on his way over here."

"You can't just keep me here," the young woman said. "That's... I don't know, kidnapping or something."

"Then give me a straight answer. What were you doing with the pizza boxes?"

The young woman looked down at the floor. "I just need them, okay?"

Ellie frowned. The dots were beginning to connect in a new way. "Have you been selling pizzas under my name?" she asked.

Sadie paled visibly. "You're crazy," she said. "Get out of my way."

"No, this is serious. This could get me in huge legal trouble. There are codes a restaurant has to follow for food safety and health. If someone thinks I've been letting you sell pizzas out of the back of your car, they could shut Papa Pacelli's down. You have no right to do that to me and everyone who works here."

"I need the extra money, okay? It seemed like an easy thing to do at the time."

Ellie was stunned at the young woman's confession. She had begun to suspect something like that was going on, but to hear it confirmed blew her away. "How long has this been going on? How have you been doing it?"

"I mean, it wasn't that hard. I got the idea when Sabrina started working here. She's always talking about how you make everything, and kept mentioning hints about your grandfather's secret recipe, and I thought it didn't sound too hard. I mean, making money by selling what's essentially bread with sauce and cheese on it? I wanted in. At first, I tried just doing it on my own, but no one wanted to buy pizzas from someone they had never heard of before."

Ellie shook her head out of amazement. Sadie made it sound so easy. It wasn't just a matter of throwing together some ingredients. She refrained from interrupting only because she wanted to hear the rest of the story.

Sadie continued. "Then I saw your business cards lying around – Sabrina brought some with her to hand out at some church retreat – and it just kind of clicked for me. I made a couple copies of them, but replaced your number with mine. I started handing them out, and I began getting calls for orders. Then of course I realized I needed a way to deliver the pizzas that wouldn't make people suspicious, so I started asking Sabrina to bring me some boxes, but after couple time she started asking questions so I stopped. That's when I began stealing the empty ones from the dumpster. It sounds gross, but I only used the clean ones. Things just kind of… evolved. I bought that light for the top my car a couple weeks ago, and it was like the world opened up. I got all the late-night orders and delivered to people who wanted pizzas outside of your normal delivery zone. Only a couple of people noticed the difference between my pizzas and yours, but I just blocked their numbers from my phone when they called to complain."

"I can't believe you did that," Ellie said. "You stole business from me."

The young woman snorted. "It's not like the restaurant's about to shut down or anything. You're doing just fine."

"That's not the point," Ellie said. "Did Sabrina know about this?"

"No. I knew I couldn't trust her. She would've told you. She was always the good one out of the two of us." The young woman looked away and scuffed her shoe across the floor, some unidentified emotion flashing across her face. Was it guilt?

Ellie felt as if her stomach had turned to lead. The second pizza box on the lawn the night of Sabrina's murder now seemed to make sense. "It was you," she breathed.

"What are you talking about?" Sadie asked, her voice suddenly cold.

"You were there the night that Sabrina died."

The other woman didn't respond immediately. Ellie saw her jaw clench. The young woman glanced away after a moment. Ellie wondered what was going through her brain.

"So what if I was?"

"You killed her, didn't you?"

"You're crazy."

"You killed your best friend because she was going to tell me what you were doing."

Sadie fell silent. Ellie continued, "that explains the weird call they made to change their order – an order that we hadn't gotten. They had called you first and ordered a pizza using your number, hadn't they? Then when they wanted to change it, they must have looked us up online instead of using the number on the fake business card you gave them. The two of you must have gotten there at the same time. Sabrina would have recognized your car, and when she saw what you were doing, she must have put two and two together. She was a smart girl."

"Just shut up," Sadie said. "You don't know what it was like. You don't know how much I needed the money. If she was a real friend, she wouldn't have threatened to turn me in."

"Sabrina was doing what was right," Ellie said. "But nothing you did was right. How do you think she must've felt in her last moments knowing that her friend –"

Sadie lurched forward, rushing for the door. Without thinking, Ellie got in front of her. The young woman collided with her, slapping her hands away as she reached for the handle. Ellie saw panic in her eyes.

She shoved Sadie away and reached for her phone, which she had left on the counter. She was too slow, and too oblivious. Before she knew what was happening, Sadie had grabbed a rolling pin and was swinging it at her. Ellie managed to jump back just in time. A second later, and she might have had a broken arm.

To her surprise, the young woman began laughing even though there were tears streaming down her face. "Talk about déjà vu," she said, half sobbing. "I killed my best friend with my bat from softball practice, now I'm attacking her boss with a rolling pin."

"Just put it down," Ellie said. "It's time to give up, Sadie. You've been caught."

The woman was too far gone to hear or care. She swung the rolling pin at Ellie again. Ellie jumped out of the way and the pin crashed onto the counter. Before Sadie could raise it again, Ellie stepped forward and wrapped her arms around the young woman, pinning her arms to her side. Sadie struggle for a moment, but Ellie had weight on her, and years of experience. A bear hug might not be the most traditional way of defending herself, but as long as it kept her from getting hit with that rolling pin, she wasn't about to complain.

Suddenly all of the fight went out of Sadie. The rolling pin fell to the floor. The young woman went limp in her arms, then started to cry into Ellie's shoulder. Ellie patted her back, not letting her go just in case she decided to try something again. She hoped that Russell made good on his word. He couldn't get there soon enough.

EPILOGUE

E llie reached for another cookie, reveling in the guilty pleasure of eating as many as she wanted. She had earned it.

"Killed by her best friend." Shannon shook her head. "If you ever get mad at me, I'd rather us talk it out than be reduced to violence like that."

"I'll just sick Bunny on you," Ellie said with a faint smile. "She's fierce, but she won't actually do much damage."

Her friend laughed. "I can deal with that. Sorry. We shouldn't be joking about this, not with what happened to Sabrina."

"It's good to smile again," Ellie said. "Thanks for coming over."

"Are you kidding me? Your grandmother's homemade chocolate chip cookies and wine? Well, in my case sparkling grape juice, but it's basically the same thing. I couldn't resist."

"It's the ultimate comfort food," Ellie said.

"I'm glad that her family's able to get closure now, but it makes me sad to think of all of the murders that go unsolved all over the country. I hate the fact that there are people like Sadie out there still walking around and enjoying their lives while their victims are dead."

"It bothers me too," the pizzeria owner said. "I know it bothers Russell too, but at least he can do something about it."

"He's not the only one that can do something about it," Shannon said. "We've both helped him a couple of times. I know he does a lot, but so do you. If it wasn't for you, Sadie might never have been caught."

"It was just chance that I happened to walk out there and see her going through the dumpster," Ellie said.

"Well, it wasn't 'just chance' that you followed her and then called Russell when you figured out what was going on. Not everyone would've done that."

Ellie smiled. "Thanks. I didn't really think about it, to be honest. I probably should've been more careful."

"There's no point in second-guessing yourself now," Shannon said. "You're fine, and that's what matters."

"I suppose it's true." The pizzeria owner sighed. "Now that everything with Sabrina his been resolved, I can't stop thinking about the second pizzeria. The grand opening is only two weeks away. I've been second-guessing myself – triple-guessing myself – and wondering if we should even be opening at all. But it's too late to change my mind. What am I going to do?"

"Ellie, it will be fine," Shannon said. "Seriously. Your food is good, and from what you said about Linda, she seems like a nice woman who is going to do everything she can to make the restaurant succeed. I really wish I could come down there with you, but I don't want to chance anything with this pregnancy."

"I understand," Ellie said. "You have to do what's right for you and your family. I'll send you lots of pictures, and maybe we can fly down on our own next year. I suppose with Nonna moving down there for half the year, I'll be visiting a lot."

"That's right," Shannon said. "She's going to be staying there until, what, March?"

"April. It's going to be so odd not having her here. Although she will come back for my wedding, of course."

"You'll have all of this space to yourself, which will be nice."

"I know," Ellie said. "I don't really know what I'm going to do with most of it, to be honest. I keep telling myself the nothing will really change, but I know it will. It's going to be lonely, living alone all the way out here."

"You'll be fine," her friend said. "It will be nice for you to have some time to yourself before you get married. Enjoy it. And remember, if anything ever gets to be too much, just give me a call and I'll come spend the night. James can deal with having the bed to himself for a night. In fact, he'll probably like having some alone time too. Once the little guy comes along, neither of us will have a moment of privacy for quite a long time."

"I know," Ellie said. "Thanks."

She smiled over at her best friend. She had so many relationships to be grateful for, and she knew that Shannon was right. She would just have to face the future and have faith that the second pizzeria would be a success. And if it wasn't, she would survive. She had so much ahead of her, including her own wedding, and she shouldn't let this one thing consume so much of her energy. She needed to focus more on living her life, and focus less on what could go wrong, because if there was one thing she had learned, worrying never prepared her for what was actually to come.

Made in the USA
Monee, IL
11 December 2019